JN288560

ニャンニャンが ほえるぞ

文：赤松 清・幸子　英訳：つじ もとこ
絵：赤松 茂・赤松 学

もくじ

ニャンニャンがほえるぞ……… 1

獣医のおじさん……… 11

子ツバメの冒険……… 19

ユウコちゃんのジョギング……… 29

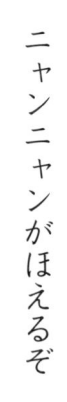

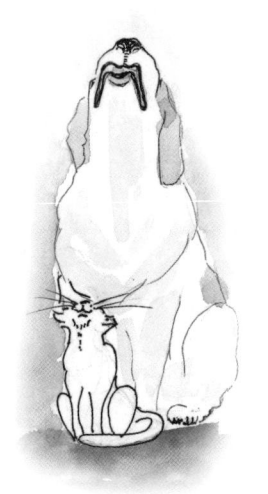

ニャンニャンがほえるぞ

大阪の郊外にある大きな病院にセントバーナード犬がいました。犬は守衛さんといっしょに病院の周囲の見まわりをしています。

セントバーナードは、スイスのアルプスで人を助ける救助犬で、肩の高さが一メートルくらいある大きな犬です。

去年のクリスマスにスイスからプレゼントされました。

それで日本の名前をクリスということにしましたが、病院の看護師さんやお炊事やお掃除の人たちはクーちゃんとよんで可愛がっていました。

犬のおうちは病院の外の金網の中にあり、小児科病棟の窓からよく見えましたので、入院している子どもたちはいつも犬をながめていました。

ある日、クーちゃんに四匹の赤ちゃんが産まれました。赤ちゃんは小さくてとてもかわいく、モゴモゴとお母さんのおなかのそばをはいまわりました。

お母さん犬のクーちゃんが大きな舌で子犬をなめると、子犬は転がって大騒動です。

小児病棟に入院中の子どもたちの中に、動物好きで頭のいいアキちゃんという十歳の男の子がいました。

ある日、アキちゃんは犬小屋を見ていてヘンなことに気づきました。子犬はお母さんと同じ白と茶色のブチが四匹だったはずなのに、今は五匹います。一匹、白い赤ちゃんがふえているのです。

アキちゃんは看護師さんにそのことを伝えました。

看護師さんは窓からいっしょにたしかめながら、

「ちょっとヘンだわね。お掃除のおじさんに調べてもらうから、あなたは

「寝ていなさい」
といってアキちゃんをベッドに寝かせ、頭をなでて出ていきました。
アキちゃんはしばらく横になって考えていましたが、犬のことが気になって、また窓のところにいってみました。
犬小屋のある金網の外におじさんが立って犬を見ていました。
アキちゃんは看護師さんが約束どおり調べてくれているのがとてもうれしくて、一心にその様子をながめていました。
おじさんが金網の中に入ろうとすると、お母さん犬のクーちゃんが「グオー」とほえて怒ります。おじさんはとても金網の中に入ることができません。
アキちゃんは心配になりました。
まもなく看護師さんがやってきて、
「わかったわ。ベッドに戻ってお話ししましょう」と、アキちゃんを寝かせつけながら、こう教えてくれました。「あのね、犬の赤ちゃん四匹のほかに、白い猫の赤ちゃんが一匹いるらしいの」

4

アキちゃんがおどろいて、
「犬が猫の赤ちゃんを産んだの？」
と聞くと、看護師さんは笑いながらいいました。
「そんなことはないわよ。犬は犬の子しか産まないの。猫の赤ちゃんはだれかが持ってきて、犬小屋の中に入れたんでしょうね」
看護師さんが行ってしまったので、アキちゃんはまた窓のところに行ってみました。
犬のお母さんは、犬の赤ちゃんにも猫の赤ちゃんにも同じようにお乳をやって、なめてあげていました。
アキちゃんは安心しながらも不思議（ふしぎ）な気持ちでした。

何日かたって、子犬も子猫も大きくなって、みんなでふざけっこをするようになりました。
猫の子は身軽で、子犬が飛びついてもヒョイとにげて木に登ったりします。
お母さん犬が「グオ」とほえると、子犬がまねをして「ブオ」とほえます。
猫の子も「ブオ」とほえます。

5

だんだんと日がすぎて、子犬は大きくなりました。

でも子猫はあまり大きくなりません。

守衛さんがお母さん犬を連れて歩くときは子犬も猫もついていきます。

子犬はお母さん犬のあとをちょこちょこたいきますが、猫は草をとびこえたり木にかけのぼったり、木の上で「ブオッ」とほえてみたりします。

守衛さんも猫がほえるぞとおどろいています。

子犬はだんだん大きくなって、肩の高さが一メートルくらいになり、お母

さん犬の大きさに近くなって、「グウォー」とほえるようになりました。

猫も「ブウォー」とほえます。

病院の人たちは猫がほえるぞとめずらしがり、看護師さんたちは「ニャンニャンがほえるぞ」といっておもしろがりました。

小児病棟の子どもたちも、木に登ってほえる猫をおもしろがって窓からながめました。

そのうちに看護師さんたちは、子どもたちがいたずらをすると「ニャンニャンがほえるぞ」といってしかるようになりました。

小児科の病棟に入院中の子どもたちは「ニャンニャンがほえるぞ」といわれると、おとなしくなって看護師さんのいうことをよく聞きます。

そのうちに子どもたちにだけでなく、大人の入院患者さんたちにも、看護師さんたちが「ニャンニャンがほえる」という言葉を使うようになりました。

「もう少し食事を食べられませんか」

7

「ほしくないんだ」
「ニャンニャンがほえますわよ」
「じゃあ、もう少し食べるか」
などというようなやりとりが聞かれるようになりました。
病院の中は「ニャンニャンがほえるぞ」という言葉で楽しく明るくなりました。
病気も早く治るようになるでしょうね。

　　　おわり

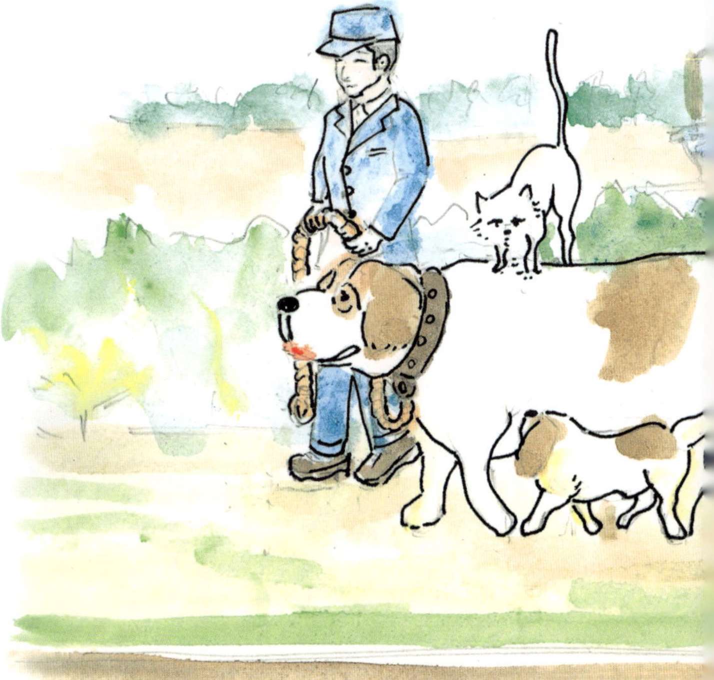

獣医のおじさん

ぼくは小学校の六年生。夏休みに、いなかのおじさんのところに遊びにいきました。

おじさんは獣医さんです。

お友だちの獣医さんといっしょに牧場を運営していて、牛を三千頭、豚を五千頭飼っています。

おじさんは子どものころから動物好きで、小学校のころはトカゲや小さいヘビを捕まえて遊んでいました。

ヘビを地面に置いて背中をなでながら「真っすぐにしなさい」と言うと、本当にヘビが真っすぐになるのがおもしろかったと教えてくれました。

おじさんのお母さんは、ズボンを洗濯機に入れるとトカゲやカエルが出てくるので、よくおどろかされました。それでもおじさんをしかることはありませんでした。お母さんも動物が好きだったのです。

おうちには犬がいました。

犬はえさをもらうお母さんよりもおじさんの言うことをよく聞きました。

おじさんは大学の農学部獣医学科に入学して、実際に獣医さんになる勉強を始めました。

でも馬や牛の世話をするのは大変です。言うことを聞かなかったり、暴れたりするときは、馬や牛は体が大きく力が強いのでとても困るのです。

牛や馬や豚に注射をしたり、薬をのませたり、レントゲン写真を撮ったり、おしっこを分析して調べたり、血液検査をしたり、図書館で調べものをしたり……と、獣医さんになるための勉強は大変です。

大学を卒業して獣医師の国家試験に合格したおじさんは、どんなお仕事を

しょうかと考えました。
獣医さんのお仕事には、街のペット病院や動物園でいろいろな動物のけがや病気を治して健康を管理するお仕事、牧場や農場で牛や豚などの出産を助けたりお乳をしぼったりするお仕事、警察犬や盲導犬の訓練所で犬が元気に訓練を受けられるようにするお仕事、保健所で牛肉や豚肉の検査をするお仕事など、いろいろなものがあります。
獣医さんになったおじさんは、ペット病院のお仕事を体験してみたり、動物園の獣医さんにお話を聞いたりして、いろいろ考えてから、牧場のお仕事をすることに決めました。

牧場にはたくさんの牛と豚がいます。
怪物のように大きな牛や豚も、かわいらしい子牛や子豚も、おじさんが牛舎や豚舎に入ってくると、首を振ったり鳴いたり、舌を出したりします。
おじさんは、動物の頭をなでたり首を軽くたたいたりして声をかけます。
「元気か、よしよし」
牛がたくさんいるので、ふんもたくさん出ます。

牛のふんはブルドーザーで集めて、わらと混ぜ、倉庫に山のように積んであります。これは肥料として畑や田んぼの土に混ぜるものです。農家の人は、稲からお米を収穫したあとのわらを牧場に持ってきます。牧場では、わらに牛のふんを混ぜて肥料を作ります。

このように、牧場と農家の間で牛のふんとわらをやりとりしながら進めていくような農業を、循環農業といいます。

別々の仕事をしている人が、自分の仕事でできてくるいらないものを、それを必要とするところにおたがいに回し合って、うまく役に立てていくのは、すばらしいことだと思いました。

牧場の子牛牛舎の子牛は、コンピュ

ーターの記録盤がついた首輪をつけています。

子牛たちは、それぞれ特別に決められた量のお乳が出る大きな哺乳びんからお乳を飲みます。

子牛が飲みすぎないように、その子牛に決められた量が終わるとお乳は出なくなります。また、お乳の成分も調節されています。

その調節は、獣医さんがコンピューターのプログラムに打ち込んで行います。

子牛は、一頭ごとに獣医さんが決めたお乳を、コンピューターで管理された哺乳びんから飲んで大きくなるのです。

子牛は獣医さんをお父さんと思い、牛舎のお掃除や体をブラシでこすったり水で洗ったりしてくれるおじさんやおばさんをお母さんだと思っているのだそうです。

大きくなった牛や豚が売られていくときは、受け取りにきたトラックに乗った牛や豚を、獣医さんや世話係のおじさんやおばさんたちが見送ります。

みんな、涙を流して手を振ります。

牛や豚も、大声で鳴きます。

16

おばさんの中には声を上げて泣く人もいます。

ぼくも涙が出ました。

おじさんがぼくの頭に手をのせて、「よしよし。おまえはお父さんやお母さんの言うことをよくきいて、うんと勉強しろよ。お父さんとお母さんを大切にしろよ」

と言いました。

涙をふきながら、ぼくは本当にそうしようと思いました。

おうちに帰ったら、お母さんがぼくの大好きなアイスクリームを作って待っていてくれました。

お母さんの顔を見たら涙が出てきたので、洗面所に行って涙をぬぐい、顔を洗いました。

それからお母さんといっしょにアイスクリームを食べました。

おわり

子ツバメの冒険

空港ビルの倉庫の軒下に、ツバメの巣がありました。

春、暖かくなると、南の国からツバメが帰ってきます。今年も二羽のツバメが帰ってきて、仲よく暮らしていました。

ある日、巣の中から「ピーピー」という鳴き声が聞こえてきました。子ツバメが生まれたのです。

次の日から親ツバメは大忙し。二羽は、ひっきりなしに飛んでいって、えさをとってきては子ツバメに食べさせます。

四、五日たつと、子ツバメが五羽、巣の端に並んでとまっているのが見かけられるようになりました。

親ツバメが帰ってくると、口を大きく開けて「ピーピーピーピー」とえさをねだります。

下を通る人はそれを見上げてほほえましい気持ちになりました。

長い羽毛（うもう）におおわれて丸っこかった子ツバメは、だんだん大きくなり、羽をバタバタさせるようになりました。

ある日、一羽の子ツバメが羽ばたいていると、自然に体が浮き上がってしまいました。

あわてて巣の端につかまろうとしても届（とど）かず、体は少しずつ降下（こうか）して、とうとう地面に降（お）り立ってしまいました。

巣を見上げましたが、とても帰れそうにありません。

向こうから猫（ねこ）がやってきました。立ち止まり、猫はすぐに子ツバメに気づきました。

頭を低くしてしのび寄ってきます。

子ツバメは猫を見たことがないので、ただピーピーと鳴いていました。

猫はだんだん近づいてきます。

そのとき、猫の鼻先を、黒いものがサッとかすめました。

猫はびっくりして飛びのきました。

それでも猫は、簡単には引き下がりません。あたりを気にしながら、ふたたび子ツバメに近づこうとします。

すると、また黒いものが飛んできて、猫を追いはらおうとします。

黒いものは親ツバメでした。

そこへフライトアテンダントのおね

えさんが通りかかりました。
「あら、小鳥」おねえさんは子ツバメを手のひらにのせて巣を見上げました。「あんた、落ちたの。困ったわね」
子ツバメは暖かい手の上で羽をバタバタさせたので、体が少し浮き上がりました。
「あんた飛べるの。それなら巣のほうに投げ上げてあげるからおうちにお帰りなさい」と、おねえさんは子ツバメを両手で包むようにして「イチ、ニのサン」と高くほうってくれました。
子ツバメの体はフワッと宙に浮きました。目の前に巣が見えたので、一生懸命に羽をばたつかせて端っこをつかみました。
ほかの子ツバメたちはピーピーと喜びま

した。
「もう落ちてはだめよ」
おねえさんは巣を見上げ、手を振って空港ビルのほうに行ってしまいました。
子ツバメは外をながめながら、目標を決めてちゃんと飛べばいいんだ、と思いました。最初は目の前の電線、次は向こうの電線、それから向うのビル、と目標を定め、思いきり羽ばたくと、勢(いきお)いよく飛び出しました。
目の前の電線にうまく飛びつきました。
子ツバメは大喜び。巣のほうを振(ふ)り返って、ほかの子ツバメたちに言いました。
「飛んでみろよ。いい気持ちだよ」
でも、ほかの子ツバメたちは、なかなか飛ぼうとしません。
子ツバメは次の電線に飛びつき、それからビルの屋上まで飛んでいきました。
ビルの屋上は広くて、ところどころに水がたまっていました。
子ツバメは水たまりの水を飲みながら飛ぶ練習をして、屋上の端から端まで飛べるようになりました。

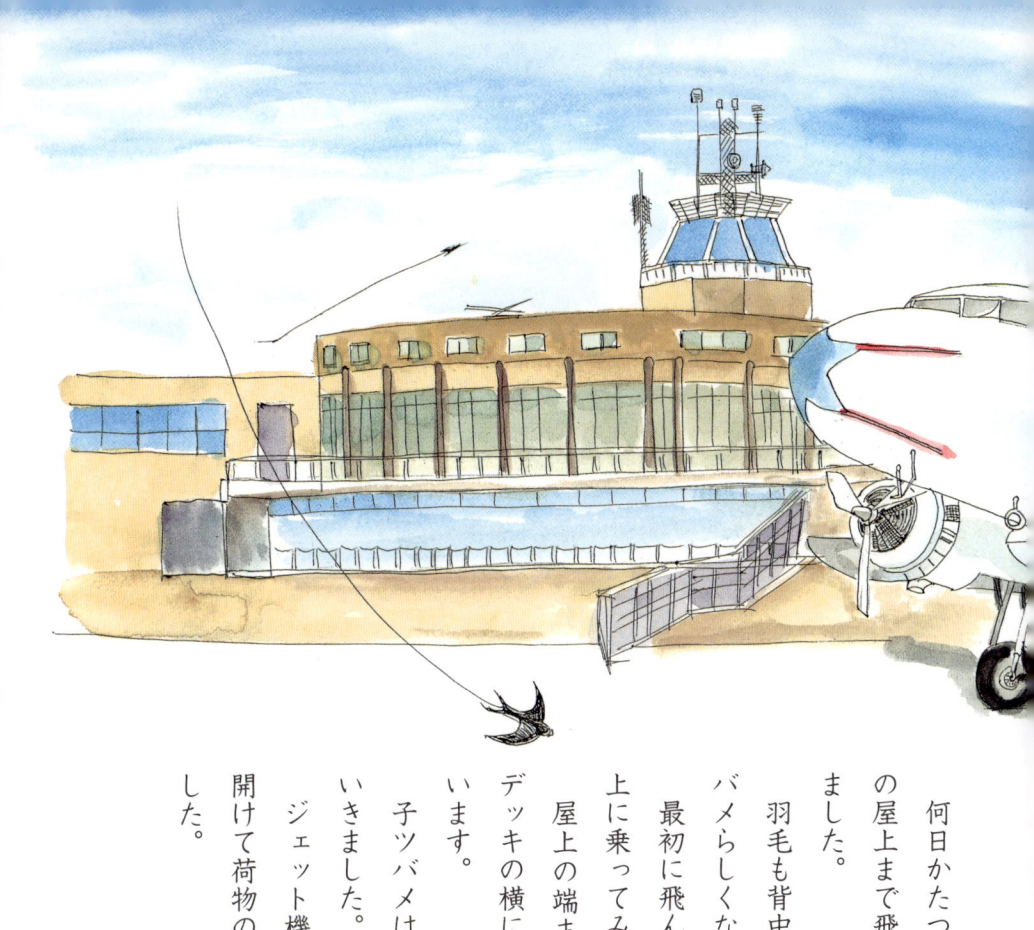

何日かたつと、子ツバメたちはみんなビルの屋上まで飛んでいって飛ぶ練習をしていました。

羽毛も背中が黒くおなかは白くなり、ツバメらしくなりました。

最初に飛んだ子ツバメは、ジェット機の上に乗ってみようと思いました。

屋上の端まで行って見下ろすと、搭乗デッキの横に大きなジェット機がとまっています。

子ツバメはジェット機の近くまで飛んでいきました。

ジェット機はとても大きくて、とびらを開けて荷物の積みこみをしているところでした。

子ツバメはジェット機の上に降り立ちましたが、そこはとてもつるつるしていて、つかむところもなく、羽をばたつかせながらすべり落ちてしまいました。

落ちたところは、このあいだのおねえさんが積みこみ作業中のお弁当の上でした。

「あら、ツバメの子」

おねえさんはおどろいて拾い上げ、手のひらにのせました。

「こら、こんなところにいると荷物につぶされるぞ」と言って、子ツバメの頭を指先でポンポンとたたきました。「エンジンに吸いこまれたら死んじゃうんだぞ」

それから、「高くほうってあげるから遠

くに飛んでいきなさい。飛行機の近くは危ないからだめ」と言って、子ツバメを投げ上げました。「イチ、二のサン」
子ツバメは目が回りました。高く浮いたあと、今度は落ち始めました。風を切って落ちるので、羽ばたくことができません。夢中で羽に力を入れて、ピンとのばしたら、子ツバメの体は空気の流れに乗り、すごいスピードで飛ぶことができました。
子ツバメは大喜びです。
次の日から、子ツバメは、飛びながら口を開けて虫を食べることや、川の水を飲む練習をしました。
木々の葉が緑色から黄色に変わり、秋になって、子ツバメたちが親ツバメといっしょに南の国に飛び立つ日が近づいてきました。
南の国に行っても、お仕事中の日本のやさしいフライトアテンダントさんに会うことがあるでしょうね。

おわり

ユウコちゃんのジョギング

ユウコちゃんは幼稚園生です。

おうちにはお父さんとお母さんとおじいちゃんと犬のタローと猫のミーがいました。

お父さんとお母さんはお勤めをしていたので、ユウコちゃんを幼稚園バスが来るところまで送っていくのもお迎えにくるのもおじいちゃんでした。幼稚園から帰っておうちで遊ぶときも、おじいちゃんといっしょでした。

ユウコちゃんはお絵かきをしたり、折り紙をしたり、お歌を歌ったり、お庭でおじいちゃんとボールを投げたりして遊びました。

おじいちゃんは毎日、犬のタローを連れて、おうちの裏の川の土手の上をジョギングしていました。おじいちゃんが走るときは、ユウコちゃんもいっしょに走りました。猫のミーもついてきました。
おじいちゃんは走るときに「よいしょ、よいしょ」とかけ声をかけます。
ユウコちゃんもいっしょに「よいしょ、よいしょ」と言って走りましたが、「よいしょ」はなんだかヘンだと思っていました。
ある日、ユウコちゃんとおじいちゃんが走っていると、高校生のおねえちゃんたちが走ってきました。おねえち

ゃんたちは、「ふぁいと、ふぁいと」とかけ声をかけて走っていきました。

ユウコちゃんは、ふぁいとはいいな、と思いました。

それで、おじいちゃんに「走るときは、ふぁいと、ふぁいと、と言うことにしようよ。よいしょはおかしいよ」と提案しました。

おじいちゃんは「ふぁいと、ふぁいとか。よし、そうしよう」と賛成しました。

それからは「ふぁいと、ふぁいと」のかけ声で走るようになりましたが、おじいちゃんは入れ歯なので「ほいと、ほいと」に聞こえました。

ユウコちゃんは元気に「はいと、はいと」と走りました。

犬のタローを連れて走るときは「わんわん」という犬の鳴き声も入ります。

猫のミーがついてくると「ほいと、はいと、わんわん、ニャオニャオ」になります。

土手を通る人たちは、そのかけ声を聞いて、にこにこほほえんでいました。

ある日、おじいちゃんとユウコちゃんはいつものようにジョギングをしていました。

その日はお空がきれいに晴れて、とても気持ちのよい日でした。

いつものように「ほいと、ほいと」「はいと、はいと」「わんわん」「ニャオニャオ」

で走っていましたが、途中でおじいちゃんが「きょうはとても気持ちがいいから、少し速く走るぞ。ユウコちゃんもがんばれよ」と言うと、いつもより速く走りだしました。

ユウコちゃんもスピードを上げました。

ユウコちゃんは途中で転んでしまいました。おひざをすりむいて、よく見ると血が出ています。

ユウコちゃんは大きな声で「おじいちゃーん、いたいよー、血が出てる」とおじいちゃんを呼びました。

おじいちゃんは引き返してきて、ユウコちゃんのおひざを手でおさえて「だいじょうぶ。痛くない、痛くない」と言ってユウコちゃんをおんぶしました。

タローの鎖を引きながら、土手から下りてお薬屋さんに行きました。お薬屋さんではおねえさんが、おひざをウェットティッシュできれいにふいてお薬を塗り、傷テープをはってくれました。

おじいちゃんが「どうだよくなったかい？　もう痛くないね」と聞いたので、ユウコちゃんはコックリとうなずきました。

33

34

おじいちゃんはお薬屋さんにお礼を言ってユウコちゃんを背負(せお)い、土手の上の道を帰りました。

ユウコちゃんはおじいちゃんの背中で夕焼けの赤いお空をながめながら「さいた、さいた、チューリップの花が」とチューリップのお歌を歌いました。

おじいちゃんが立ち止まって「ユウコちゃん、お歌が出ればもうだいじょうぶ。歩こうか?」と聞きました。

ユウコちゃんは「いや、おんぶがいい」と返事をしました。

「そうか」と言っておじいちゃんはまた歩き始めました。

遠くのほうから「おじいちゃーん、ユウコちゃーん」という声が聞こえてきました。

よく見ると、土手の先のほうにお母さんとお父さんがいました。

ユウコちゃんはとてもうれしくて、おじいちゃんの背中から手を振って「お母さーん」と大きな声で呼びました。
お母さんとお父さんが、手を振りながら急いでやってきます。
おじいちゃんはタローの鎖を放しました。タローは鎖を引きずってお父さんのほうに走っていきました。
ユウコちゃんもおじいちゃんの背中から下り、おひざが少し痛いのをがまんして、お母さんのほうに走っていきました。
「ユウコちゃんどうしたの、だいじょうぶ？」と言って、お母さんが抱き上げてくれました。
「転んでひざをすりむいてしまったから、薬屋さんに寄って傷テープをはってもらったんだ」と、おじいちゃんが説明しました。「きれいに消毒して薬も塗ってもらったから、もうだいじょうぶ」
「おじいちゃん、お世話になりました」とお母さん。「ユウコちゃん、おじいちゃんによくしてもらってよかったね」
ユウコちゃんはお母さんにおんぶしてもらって、犬のタローはお父さんに鎖を引い

36

てもらって、おじいちゃんとみんなで土手の道をゆっくり、おうちに向かいました。お空はきれいな夕焼けで、川も土手も、うす赤色に染まって見えました。ユウコちゃんはお母さんの背中に顔をくっつけてみました。暖かくていいにおいがしました。ユウコちゃんは、いつまでもお母さんとこうしていたいなと思いました。

次の朝、いつものように幼稚園バスまでおじいちゃんに送ってもらうとき、ユウコちゃんはおじいちゃんに聞きました。
「みんなお母さんが送ってくるのに、ユウコだけどうしておじいちゃんなの？」
おじいちゃんが「お母さんはお勤めがあるからだよ」と答えると、なぜかむずかしそうな顔をしていました。

その日のジョギングを、ユウコちゃんは足が痛いと言ってお休みしました。おじいちゃんが一人、タローをつれて走りました。

その夜、おじいちゃんとお父さんとお母さんは相談をしました。そして、ユウコちゃんが小学校に行くまでの間、お母さんはお勤めをお休みすることになりました。

次の日はお母さんが幼稚園バスのお見送りにいきました。

ユウコちゃんはとてもうれしくて、お母さんの手をにぎってぶら下がりながら歩きました。バスに乗ってきた幼稚園の先生に「先生、きょうはお母さんがお見送りに来てるの」と、ぴょんぴょん飛びはねながら教えてあげました。お母さんもにこにこ先生にごあいさつをしました。

その日はバスのお出迎えにもお母さんが来ました。

ユウコちゃんはびっくりして、とてもうれしかったのですが、おじいちゃんはどうして来ないのかなとちょっぴり心配になりました。

おうちに帰ったユウコちゃんは、おじいちゃんに「きょうはどうして幼稚園バスのお迎えにこなかったの？」と聞きました。

おじいちゃんは「お母さんが行ったからいいだろう」と答えましたが、ユウコちゃんは「よくないよ、おじいちゃんが来なくちゃいやだ。あしたはおじいちゃん来てよ」とせがみました。

おじいちゃんは「わかったわかった、あすはおじいちゃんがお迎えに行くよ」と返事をしました。

ユウコちゃんは「約束だよ」と言って、おじいちゃんの顔をのぞきこみました。

おじいちゃんは、なんだかうれしそうに笑っていました。

次の日はお母さんが幼稚園バスのお見送りに行って、おじいちゃんがお迎えに行きました。

ユウコちゃんは、みんなが約束を守ってくれたのでとてもうれしく思いました。

おうちに帰るとお母さんがジュースとホットケーキを作って待っていました。ユウコちゃんはおじいちゃんといっしょにジュースを飲んでホットケーキを食べました。食べ終わると、ユウコちゃんは「おじいちゃんジョギングに行こう」と言いました。おじいちゃんはおどろいて、「足は痛くないのか？」と聞きましたが、ユウコちゃんは「うん、幼稚園でもお走りをしたよ」と平気そうでした。それから「お母さんもジョギングしようよ」と誘いました。

お母さんは「そうね、ごいっしょしましょうか。ちょっと待ってね」と言うと、トレーニングウェアに着替えてきました。

おじいちゃんとユウコちゃんとお母さんと犬のタローと猫のミーの三人と二匹のジョギングが始まりました。

おじいちゃんの「ほいと」のあとに、ユウコちゃんの「はいと」、その次にお母さんの「ふぁいと」、タローのワンワン、猫のニャオが続いて、「ほいと、はいと、ふぁいと、ワンワン、ニャオ」になりました。ユウコちゃんはうれしくて、大きな声で「はいと、はいと」とかけ声をかけて走りました。お母さんはきれいな声で「ふぁいと、ふぁいと」、おじいちゃんも元気な声で「ほいと、ほいと」と走りました。ユウコちゃんはうれしくて、きょうはいい日だなーと思いました。
お父さんがお勤めから帰ってきて、みんなで夕ごはんを食べているとき

に、ユウコちゃんはきょうのジョギングのことをお話しして「お父さんもお休みのときには、みんなといっしょに走ろうよ」と誘いました。
お母さんが「それはいいわね」と言いました。
お父さんはちょっと考えてから「うん、みんなで走ろう。あしたは土曜日でお休みだからさっそく走ろうか」と言いました。
ユウコちゃんは「ばんざーい、あしたはみんなで走るんだ」と大喜びしました。

次の日、朝ごはんのあと、お父さんのトレーナーやジョギング用のお靴を準備(じゅんび)して、走るのはお昼ごはんがすんでからということになりました。お母さんはお茶を冷蔵庫(れいぞうこ)で冷やしたり、今度はそれをペットボトルにつめ替えたりと、準備に大忙(おおいそ)がしです。
ようやくみんなで走り始めましたが、お父さんのかけ声は「がんばれ、がんばれ」です。
みんなのかけ声は「ほいとほいと、はいとはいと、ふぁいとふぁいと、ガンバレガンバレ、ワンワン、ニャーオ」になりました。
みんな元気に大きな声を出して走り

ました。ユウコちゃんはうれしくて、またとてもおもしろくて、汗もいっぱいかきました。
ジョギングが終わっておうちに帰り、おふろに入ったあと、みんなで気持ちよくお昼寝をしました。お昼寝のあともユウコちゃんは、きょうはよかったなーとジョギングのことを思い出して、にこにこしていました。
それからは、土曜日と日曜日のお父さんがお休みの日は、みんなでジョギングをすることになりました。
いつも楽しいジョギングでした。

夏が過ぎて秋になりました。入道雲が消えて、秋晴れの澄んだお空にはけ雲が浮かぶ、気持ちのよいジョギングびよりが続きました。

十一月になると、ユウコちゃんは自分のお誕生日のことを考えました。ユウコちゃんのお誕生日は十一月の十日です。お誕生日のお祝いに買ってもらいたいものがあるのです。

それはおつくえといす、ランドセルと鉛筆、クレヨン、靴やお洋服——小学校の一年生になる準備のお道具です。ほしいものがたくさんあるので、どうしようか迷いました。

ユウコちゃんのお誕生日の十一月十日になりました。お誕生日のケーキをお母さんが作りました。ローソクが六本立っていました。みんなが「ハッピーバースデーユウコちゃん」と歌って、ユウコちゃんがローソクを吹き消しました。みんなが手をたたきました。

おじいちゃんが「ユウコちゃんおめでとう。もうすぐ一年生だね」と、紙に包んだ

プレゼントを渡してくれました。
お父さんからもプレゼントをもらいました。
お母さんもにっこりほほえんでプレゼントを渡してくれました。
ユウコちゃんはとてもうれしくて、すぐにプレゼントを開けてみました。
おじいちゃんのプレゼントはクレヨンとお絵かき帳と鉛筆でした。
お母さんのプレゼントは赤いお洋服でした。
お父さんのプレゼントはお靴でした。
みんなユウコちゃんがほしかったものばかりでした。
ユウコちゃんは立ち上がって「ありがとうございました」と、ていねいにおじぎをしました。
おじいちゃんとお父さんとお母さんがパチパチと拍手してくれました。
おじいちゃんが「ちゃんとごあいさつができた。えらいえらい」とほめてくれま

した。
ケーキを切ってみんなで食べているとき、おじいちゃんが「ユウコちゃんは大きくなったらなんになるの？」と聞きました。
ユウコちゃんはしばらく考えてから、「ユウコはね、お薬屋さんのおねえさんになるの」と答えました。
するとお父さんが「それなら、お医者さんになるか」と聞きました。
ユウコちゃんは「いやだよ、お注射をしたら血が出るよ。ユウコはお注射はきらい」と言いました。
お母さんが「幼稚園の先生はどう？」とたずねました。
ユウコちゃんは「いたずらっ子が言うことを聞かないに、しかんなきゃいけないから困（こま）るよ」と言いました。
おじいちゃんが「よしよし、いろんなことを考えているユウコちゃんはえらい」と言ったら、お父さんもお母さんも「ほんとにえらいね」とほめてくれました。
ユウコちゃんは、ほめられたのはうれしかったのですが、まだ心配事がありました。
「来年は一年生になるから、お勉強のつくえといすとランドセルがいるの」

おじいちゃんが「そうだそうだ、ずっと先の話より来年が大事だ。お勉強のおつくえといすとランドセルはおじいちゃんが買ってやる。お正月を過ぎたらユウコちゃんといっしょに買いに行こう」と言いました。
「約束だよ」と念をおして、ユウコちゃんはやっと安心しました。
その日のお夕飯は、お誕生祝いのお赤飯（せきはん）と、大好きなオムレツとハンバーグでしたが、ユウコちゃんはお誕生ケーキを食べたのであまり食べられませんでした。
お父さんといっしょのおふろのあと、お布団（ふとん）に入って、きょうはいいお誕生日、と思い返しました。プレゼントをもらったし、おつくえといすとランドセルを買ってもらうお約束もしたし、お薬屋のおねえさんになることも伝えたし。そうして安心して眠（ねむ）りにつきました。

次の日の朝、ユウコちゃんは幼稚園バスまでお母さんと手をつないでいきました。

途中でお友だちに会いました。お友だちもお母さんと手をつないで歩いていました。
「おはよう」とお友だちに声をかけ、お母さんどうしもごあいさつ。みんなでお話しをしながら歩きました。

今まで、ユウコちゃんは、いつもおじいちゃんと二人で歩いていました。けさはお友だちやお友だちのお母さんといっしょにお話しをしながら歩けたので、とてもうれしい気持ちでした。やっとお友だちと同じになったような気がしたのです。

幼稚園ではお絵かきの勉強がありました。
先生が一人ひとりに大きなお絵かきの紙を配って言いました。
「何でも好きな絵を紙いっぱいに大きくかきましょう」
先生も紙を壁にはり付けて、運動会のお走りの大きな絵をかきました。
ユウコちゃんはそれを見て、自分もジョギングの絵をかきました。先生の絵を考えながらかくと、自分でもうまくかけました。
お空は夕焼けにすることにしました。お空に赤いクレヨンを薄く塗りました。夕焼け空ができあがりました。
先生がユウコちゃんの絵を見て「上手だわ」とほめてくれました。

ユウコちゃんは「おじいちゃんとお父さんとお母さんと私と犬のタローと猫のミーでジョギングしたの。夕焼けでお空が赤くなって、まわりも赤くなっていたの」と説明しました。

先生は、「お空が赤いのはよくわかるけど、クレヨンでは赤で塗るよりもオレンジ色を使うほうがきれいになるの。ユウコちゃんの絵は赤色を塗ってあるから、その上に黄色を薄く塗って色を混ぜるとよくなるわよ。先生、やってみようか？」と言って、黄色とオレンジ色のクレヨンでユウコちゃんのかいた絵の上を薄くぬりました。まわりで見ていたほかの先生やお友だちが「ウワー！」と声を出しておどろくほど、夕焼け空がきれいになりました。

ユウコちゃんはクレヨンの色を混ぜて塗る方法があることを知りました。

幼稚園バスで帰ると、おじいちゃんがお迎えにきて待っていてくれました。ユウコちゃんはおじいちゃんが約束を守ってくれているのがとてもうれしくて「おじいちゃんお迎えありがとう」とお礼を言いました。

おじいちゃんはうれしそうに笑って「約束だからね」と言いました。

ユウコちゃんは、約束は大事なんだ、と思いました。
おじいちゃんといっしょにおうちに帰ると、ユウコちゃんは絵を取り出して見せました。
おじいちゃんがおどろいて「ユウコちゃんは絵が上手だね。夕焼けの空はみごとだ」とほめてくれました。
お母さんも「ユウコちゃんは絵が上手なんだなあ。うん、夕焼けの空も美しくかけてるもの。夕焼けの空も美しくかけてるもの。
おじいちゃんがどこからか写真の額を持ってきて、ガラスの入った額縁の中のユウコちゃんの絵は、本当にきれいに見えました。
おじいちゃんはその絵をリビングの壁にかけました。
いすに座って絵をながめ「なかなかいいぞ」と喜びました。
お父さんがお勤めから帰ると、お母さんがさっそくこのことをお知らせしました。
「ユウコちゃんが幼稚園で、ジョギングの絵を上手に描いたんですよ」と、リビングの絵を指さしました。
「そうか」と言って何げなく絵を見たお父さんはおどろきました。

50

絵の近くまで行って見て、はなれて見て、いすに座って見て、「ユウコは画才があるのかな、だれに似たのかな」と首をひねりました。
そして「上手にかけたね」とほめてくれました。
その夜、ユウコちゃんはお布団の中で考えました。
きょう、おじいちゃんにもお母さんにもお父さんにも絵が上手だとほめられたけど、先生が直した夕焼けがよかったんだ、と。
あしたから幼稚園でいろんな勉強をして、次は小学校、中学校、高校、大学に行ってももっともっと勉強しなければならない。それはとても時間がかかるし、とても大変なことだ。
でも、自分はそれをしなければならないし、絶対やるんだ。そう思うと勇気がわいてくるようでした。
そうしてユウコちゃんは眠りにつきました。

　　　おわり

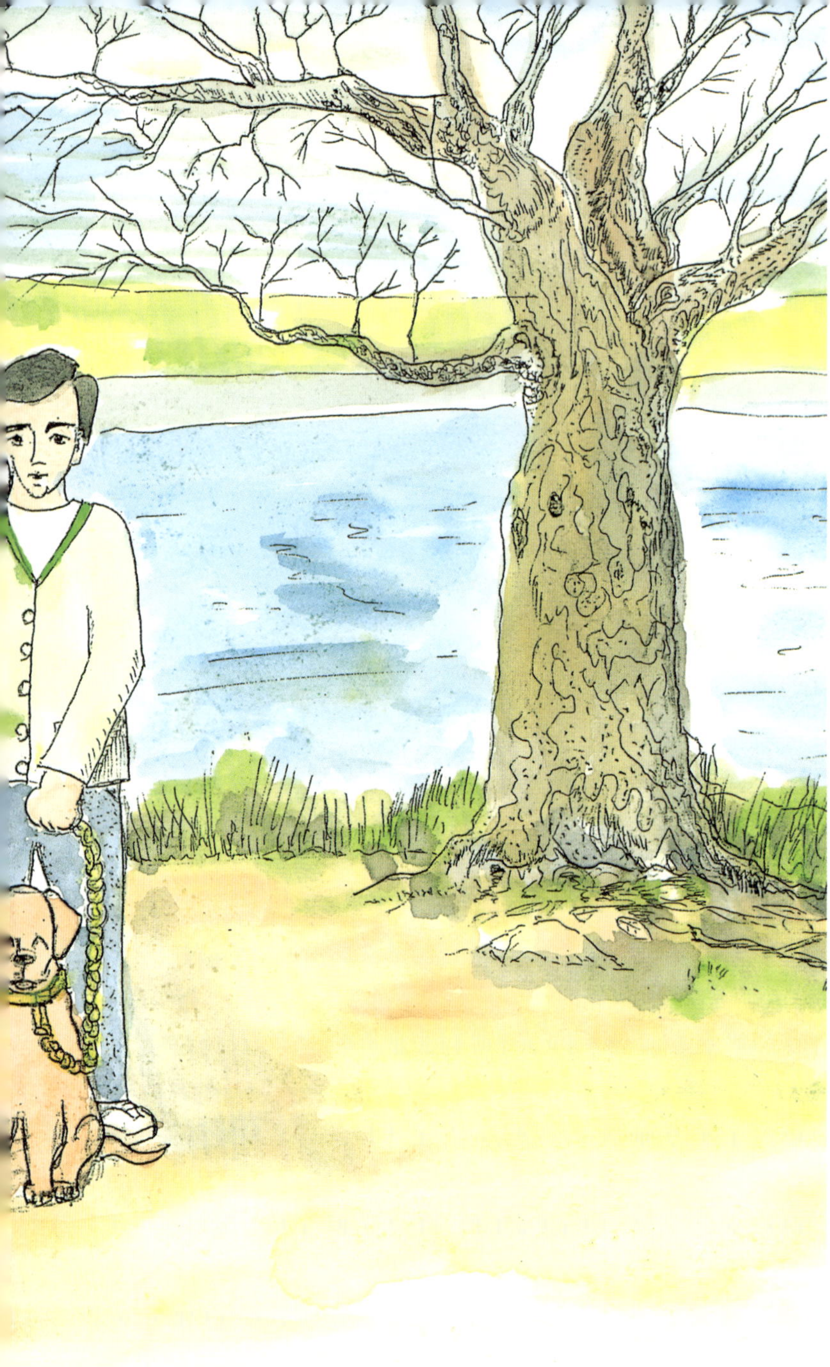

53

you should use the color orange instead of red. Now you can spread yellow lightly over the red sunset you've drawn so that the two colors will be mixed. Let me show you how." Then she drew the sunset lightly over the red one with yellow and orange crayon. The sunset in the picture became so beautiful that the other teachers and the children who had been watching exclaimed, "Wow!" Until then, Yuko-chan hadn't known about the way to create a new color by mixing colors.

That day when Yuko-chan got off the kindergarten bus, she found Grandpa waiting for her. Yuko-chan was happy that Grandpa had kept his promise. She said, "Thank you for coming to meet me, Grandpa." Smiling happily, Grandpa said, "I made a promise, didn't I?" Yuko-chan knew how important it was to keep promises. When they came home, Yuko-chan took out her picture and showed it to Grandpa. "You drew really well," said Grandpa in surprise. "The sunset in the picture is wonderful." Mommy said, "Yuko-chan is really good at drawing. The sunset in the picture is really beautiful."

Grandpa found a frame with a photograph in it. He took the photograph out of the frame, and put Yuko-chan's picture in it. The picture in the frame looked really beautiful. Grandpa hung the picture on the wall in the living room. Sitting in a chair, he said, "What a good picture!"

Daddy came home from work. When Mommy said, pointing to the picture, "Yuko-chan drew a picture at kindergarten and brought it home." he just said, "Oh?" But when he saw the picture in the frame, Daddy looked really surprised. Watching the picture, first he got closer, and then stepped back, and after that sat in a chair. "Yuko-chan has talent for art, doesn't she? I wonder who she inherited it," said Daddy. "You drew very well," said Daddy, looking at Yuko-chan.

That night Yuko-chan kept thinking in bed. "Grandpa, Mommy and Daddy praised me for my drawing, but if the teacher hadn't helped me with the color of the sunset, that wouldn't have been such a good drawing. I still have a lot of things to learn at kindergarten. After I finish kindergarten, I'll have to keep learning at elementary school, junior high school, senior high school, and college. It takes a lot of time and effort, but I have to do that. I definitely will." Feeling hopeful and encouraged, Yuko-chan went to sleep.

The End

injection and see blood. I hate injections." said Yuko-chan. Mommy said, "How about a kindergarten teacher?" "I don't want to have to scold mischievous boys," said Yuko-chan. Grandpa said, "All right. What a wise girl you are to be able to think carefully about your future!" Daddy and Mommy said, "You really are." Though she were happy about their kind words, Yuko-chan said, "There are other things I really need. They are a desk at which I can study, a chair and a school backpack." Grandpa said, "You are right. We should pay more attention to things you need next year rather than your distant future. All right. I'll buy you a desk, a chair and a school backpack. After New Year's Day is over, let's go out for the shopping." "Promise?" said Yuko-chan and felt relived at last. The dinner for the day were festive red bean rice and Yuko-chan's favorite, omelets and hamburger steak. Yuko-chan couldn't eat much because she had eaten the birthday cake and was not hungry enough. "Save them for me until tomorrow," said Yuko-chan. Then she took a bath with Daddy, brushed her teeth and went to bed. Yuko-chan kept thinking about what had happened that day in bed. "I enjoyed my birthday a lot. I got a lot of presents. Grandpa made a promise to buy me a desk, a chair and a school backpack. I told them that I would be a pharmacist." She felt relieved and fell asleep.

Next morning, Yuko-chan went to the kindergarten bus with Mommy, holding her hand. Yuko-chan saw one of her friends on the way. She was walking hand in hand with her mother, too. Yuko-chan said to her, "Good morning." Mommy greeted her and her mother, saying "Good morning" Then they began to walk together, talking with each other. Until then Yuko-chan had always been with Grandpa, so she was really glad that she was walking with Mommy, talking with her friend and her mother.

At kindergarten, there was a period for drawing. The teacher handed out large drawing paper and said, "Draw a picture of whatever you like all over the paper." Then the teacher put a piece of paper on the wall and drew a large picture of children running on a sports day. After watching the picture on the wall, Yuko-chan drew a picture of the jogging with her family. She thinly painted the picture with a red crayon and drew the sunset sky. While drawing, the picture on the wall helped Yuko-chan a lot.

Looking at Yuko-chan's picture, the teacher said, "Good Job, Yuko-chan." Yuko-chan said, "Grandpa, Daddy, Mommy, Taro the dog and Mie the cat went jogging. The sky was red, and everything around us was red, too." The teacher said, "You can say that the color of the sunset sky is red, but when you draw a sunset,

Next day they planned to go jogging after finishing lunch. After finishing breakfast, they prepared a sweatshirt and sneakers for Daddy. Mommy put tea she had made in the refrigerator and poured it into a plastic bottle so that they could take and drink it while jogging. Then they started running. Daddy ran, repeating "*Ganbare! Ganbare!*" They all kept repeating "Hoito! Hoito! Haito! Haito! Fight! Fight! *Ganbare! Ganbare!* Bowwow! Bowwow! Meow! Meow!" They all ran, shouting in a cheerful voice. Yuko-chan was so happy. She sweated a lot. After they finished jogging, they went home, took a bath and took a nap together. When she woke up, Yuko-chan thought about the jogging and how much she had enjoyed the day and smiled.

From the day on, they started to go jogging together on Saturdays and Sundays, when Daddy was off. Each time they jogged, they had a lot of fun.

Summer was over and autumn came. The sky with thunderclouds turned into that with cottony clouds. Pleasant days which was suitable for jogging lasted.

In November Yuko-chan started to think about her birthday. Her birthday is on November 10th. There were a few things Yuko-chan wanted for her birthday. They were a desk, a chair, a school backpack, pencils, crayon, shoes, clothes and things like that—she needed these things to go to elementary school. Since there are so many she wanted, she was not sure of getting all of them.

It was November 10th, her birthday. Mommy made a birthday cake with six candles on it.

Everybody else sang, "Happy birthday, Yuko-chan!" When Yuko-chan blew off the candles, they clapped their hands. "Happy birthday, Yuko-chan. School starts soon, doesn't it?" said Grandpa and he handed her his present wrapped in paper. Daddy also gave her a present. Mommy gave her a present with a smile on her face. Yuko-chan was so happy that she couldn't wait to open them. Grandpa's presents were crayon, a sketchpad, and pencils. Mommy's were red clothes. Daddy's was a pair of shoes. They were all what Yuko-chan had wanted. Yuko-chan stood up and said, "Thank you very much for the presents," and bowed before them. Grandpa, Daddy and Mommy clapped their hands for her. Grandpa said, "You are such a good girl to be able to thank us."

After that they cut the cake and started to eat it. Grandpa said to Yuko-chan, "What do you want to be when you grow up?" After thinking for a while, she said, "I want to be a pharmacist working at a pharmacy." Daddy said, "How about a doctor?" "No, I don't want to be a doctor. If I become a doctor, I'll have to give an hurt any more?" "No, it doesn't. I did a little running while I was in kindergarten today", said Yuko-chan. Then she said to Mommy, "Why don't you join us in jogging, Mommy?" "All right. I will. But before we go, give me a minute", Mommy said and left. After a while, She came back in her sweatpants.

The three persons and the two animals—Grandpa, Yuko-chan, Mommy, Taro the dog, and Mie the cat—started jogging. Grandpa said, "Hoit!" After that Yuko-chan said, "Haito!" After that Mommy said, "Fight!" And then Taro barked, "Bowwow!" Mie meowed, "Meow!" "Hoito! Haito! Fight! Bowwow! Meow!" Yuko-chan was so happy. She ran, repeating "Haito! Haito!" Mommy repeated in a beautiful voice, "Fight! Fight!" Grandpa also repeated in a cheerful voice, "Hoito! Hoito!" Yuko-chan really enjoyed jogging with her family.

Daddy came home from work. While they were sitting around the dinner table, Yuko-chan talked about how much the three of them had enjoyed jogging that day, and said to Daddy, "Why don't you join us when you have a holiday, Daddy?" Looking at Daddy, Mommy said, "That sounds like a good idea." He seemed to be thinking for a while, and said, "All right. Why don't we all go for a jog together? Tomorrow is Saturday and that's my day off. I'll join you tomorrow." Yuko-chan got excited and said, "Hooray! We're all going to go jogging together tomorrow!"

Mommy greeted the teacher with a smile on her face. That day Mommy came to the bus stop again to meet Yuko-chan. Although Yuko-chan was pleasantly surprised, she couldn't help wondering why Grandpa hadn't come to meet her. When she came home, Yuko-chan went over to Grandpa and said, "How come you didn't come to meet me at the bus stop?" Grandpa said, "Aren't you happy enough that Mommy came to meet you?" Yuko-chan said, "I am not. I wanted you to come. Be sure to come to meet me tomorrow, will you?" Grandpa said, "All right. Tomorrow I'll come to meet you." Looking Grandpa in the face, Yuko-chan said, "Promise?" Somehow, Grandpa looked kind of happy. After a while, Grandpa asked Yuko-chan if she'd like to go for a jog. Since she still had a pain in her knee, she decided to stay home. Grandpa went running with Taro.

Next day Mommy took Yuko-chan to the kindergarten bus to see her off in the morning and Grandpa came to meet her in the afternoon. Yuko-chan was happy because Mommy and Grandpa did as she had asked them to do. She couldn't help smiling. When she came home, Yuko-chan found Mommy waiting for them. She had cooked juice and hotcakes for them. Yuko-chan and Grandpa drank juice and ate hotcakes. After they finished eating, Yuko-chan said, "Why don't we go for a jog, Grandpa?" With a surprised look on his face, Grandpa said, "Doesn't your leg hurt any more, does it?" Yuko-chan shook her head.

Thanking the pharmacist for her kindness, Grandpa paid for the service. He left there with Yuko-chan on his back. He went up the bank of the river and started to walk toward the house. Looking at the flaming sunset sky on Grandpa's back, Yuko-chan sang the song "Tulip". "The tulips are in bloom!" Then Grandpa stopped and said, "You must be feeling much better to be able to sing a song. Would you rather walk?" Yuko-chan said, "No. I much prefer being on your back." He said, "All right" and started to walk again. After a while she heard Mommy calling out from a distance. "Grandpa! Yuko-chan!" When she strained her eyes, she saw Mommy and Daddy standing in the distance. Yuko-chan was so happy that she raised her hand on Grandpa's back and called Mommy in a loud voice. Waving their hands, Mommy and Daddy came running toward Grandpa. Grandpa released the dog's leash. Taro started to run over to Daddy, dragging the leash. Yuko-chan got down from Grandpa's back and started to run toward Mommy, feeling some pain in her knee. Mommy said, "What's happened, Yuko-chan? Are you all right?" Then she held Yuko-chan in her arms. Grandpa said to Mommy, "Yuko-chan fell down and grazed her knee. I took her to the pharmacy on the way and pharmacists took good care of her. One of the pharmacists disinfected the graze and applied medicine and an adhesive plaster to it, so there is nothing to worry about." Mommy said, "Thank you very much, Grandpa. You are lucky to have such a kind grandpa, Yuko-chan." Then they started to walk slow along the bank of the river toward the house—Mommy was carrying Yuko-chan on her back. Daddy was holding the dog's leash. The river and the banks of the river were also dyed light red by the sunset. Yuko-chan tried to press her head against Mommy's back. She felt warm on Mommy's back. It smelled really good. Yuko-chan hoped to be with Mommy like that forever.

Next morning, as Grandpa was taking Yuko-chan to the kindergarten bus as usual, Yuko-chan said, "I am wondering. Everybody else is with their mothers. How come I'm always with Grandpa, not Mommy?" Grandpa said, "That's because Mommy has a job." Yuko-chan noticed a serious look on his face. That day Yuko-chan didn't jog since she had a pain in her knee. Grandpa went for a jog with Taro. That night Grandpa, Daddy and Mommy had a long talk and decided that Mommy stopped working until Yuko-chan got into elementary school.

So the next morning, Mommy took Yuko-chan to the bus stop. Yuko-chan was glad about walking hand in hand with Mommy. Jumping and smiling happily, Yuko-chan said to the kindergarten teacher, "Today Mommy is here to see me off."

Yuko-chan and Jogging

Yuko-chan was a kindergartener. She lived with Daddy, Mommy, Grandpa, Taro the dog and Mie the cat. Since both Mommy and Daddy had jobs, Grandpa was the one who took her to where the kindergarten bus stopped and saw her off in the morning and met her at the same place in the afternoon. After Yuko-chan came back from kindergarten, Grandpa was always with her. Yuko-chan enjoyed drawing, folding paper, singing, and playing with a ball with Grandpa in the garden. Everyday Grandpa went for a jog with Taro the dog. He jogged along the bank of the river behind the house. Whenever Grandpa went jogging, Yuko-chan went with him. So did Mie the cat. While running, Grandpa repeated, "*Yoisho! Yoisho!*" Yuko-chan also repeated, "*Yoisho! Yoisho!*", though she had always thought it somewhat strange to say "*Yoisho! Yoisho!*"

One day while Yuko-chan and Grandpa were jogging together, they saw several senior high school girls running toward them. The girls passed by, repeating "Fight! Fight!" Yuko-chan thought it was a good idea to say, "Fight, Fight!", So she said to Grandpa, "Why don't we start repeating "Fight! Fight!", while jogging? "*Yoisho! Yoisho!*" is kind of strange." "Fight! Fight! That sounds great. Let's do it", said Grandpa. So next time they jogged, they started to repeat "Fight! Fight!" However, since Grandpa wore dentures, his voice sounded like, "Hoito! Hoito!" Yuko-chan repeated,"Haito! Haito!" in a cheerful voice. When they went for a jog with Taro, it barked, "Bowwow! Bowwow!" while running. When Mie joined them, it meowed while running. "Hoito! Hoito!" "Haito! Haito!" "Bowwow! Bowwow!" "Meow! Meow!" People walking along the bank couldn't help smiling when they heard the sounds.

One day, Grandpa and Yuko-chan were jogging as usual. It was such a nice day and there was no cloud in the sky. They were running, repeating "Hoito! Hoito!" "Haito! Haito!" "Bowwow! Bowwow!" "Meow! Meow!" While jogging, Grandpa said, "It's such a pleasant day. Let's run a little faster. Try to keep up, Yuko-chan." Then he started running fast. While runing, Yuko-chan fell down and grazed her knee. When she looked closely, she noticed it bleeding. Yuko-chan called out, "Grandpa! It hurts! My knee's bleeding!" Turning back, Grandpa looked at her knee, pressed it and said, "That's O.K. It does not hurt." Holding a leash in one hand that Taro was kept on, he carried Yuko-chan on his back. They went down from the bank they had been jogging along and went to a pharmacy. A young female pharmacist wiped Yuko-chan's knee with a wet tissue and applied medicine and an adhesive plaster to the graze. Then Grandpa said to Yuko-chan, "Do you feel any better? It doesn't

Yuko-chan and Jogging

A few days later, all the little swallows flew to the roof of the building and practiced flying there. The down of their backs had gotten black, and that of their bellies white. They looked much more like swallows. The little swallow who had flown first was thinking of flying to a jet plane. He flew to the edge of the roof of the building and tried to see what was going on at the airport. There was a huge jet plane beside the boarding gate. The little swallow got close to the jet plane. Luggage was loaded into the jet plane. The little swallow stepped on the plane, flapping his wings. The surface of the plane was slippery, and there was nothing to hold on to there. So the little swallow slid from the plane while flapping his wings.

It was on the lunch boxes a flight attendant was loading onto the plane that the little swallow fell. She picked up the little swallow and said, "Oh, a little swallow!" in surprise. She put the little swallow on her hand and said, patting the head of the little swallow with her fingertips, "See? You could have gotten killed by getting crushed or sucked into the jet's engines." And then she said, "I will throw you up, so fly far away. Don't come close to airplanes again. It's dangerous." and then she threw the little swallow up, saying "One, two, three." The little swallow got dizzy and began to fall after he was thrown high up in the sky. Because he was pushing against the wind, it was hard for him to move his wings. But when he strained and extended his wings desperately, his body floated in the flow of the air and he began to fly fast. The little swallow was delighted.

The next day the little swallow began to practice eating worms with his mouth open while flying and drinking water of the river.

The green leaves of the trees turned yellow. Autumn has come. It won't be long before the little swallows fly back to the southern country with their parent swallows. They may get to see kind flight attendants from Japan in the country.

The End

Looking outside, the little swallow thought that it was important to set a goal when he flew. The first goal the little swallow set was an electric wire in front of him. The second goal was an electric wire a little farther away. The third goal was a high building across from the nest. Setting a goal, the little swallow flapped his wings while holding on to the edge of the nest, left the nest, and reached the electric wire in front of him. The little swallow got so excited and looked toward the nest and said to the other little swallows, "Why don't you fly? It feels great." The other swallows looked scared. The little swallow flew to another electric wire, and then reached the roof of the building across from the nest. The roof of the building was large, and there were puddles here and there. The little swallow practiced flying on the roof, drank water there, and learned to fly across the roof.

The Adventure of a Little Swallow

There used to be a swallows' nest built under the eaves of the shed in an airport buildings. Every spring when it starts to get warm, swallows fly back from a southern country. That year a pair of swallows had come back and were living at peace with each other. One day there was a peep coming from the nest. Baby swallows were born.

The next day the two swallows busy flitting about to get food and giving it to their babies. A few days later, the five baby swallows began sitting side by side in the nest. When their parents came back, the five of them opened their mouths and chirped. People who were passing by looked up at the baby swallows and smiled.

The baby swallows all looked like balls covered with down, they learned to flap their wings as they grew. One day while one of the baby swallows was fluttering his wings, his body happened to float. Though he tried hard to grab the edge of the nest, he began to fall down and finally reached the ground. The little swallow looked up at the nest, which he couldn't possibly get back to for himself.

Just then a cat was passing by. When the cat noticed the little swallow, it stopped, lowered its head and got close to the little swallow. Since the little swallow had never seen cats, he kept chirping. The cat got closer and closer. Just then something black flew past its face. The cat was startled and stepped back. Looking around, the cat began to approach the little swallow again. Then again something black flew past its face, and the cat stepped back. Something black was the parent swallow.

Just then, a flight attendant was coming. She noticed the little swallow and said, "Oh, a little bird!" She put the little swallow on her hand and looked up at the nest. "You seem to have fallen from the nest. I wonder what I can do for you." The little swallow flapped his wings in the warm hand, and his body floated a little. The flight attendant said, "Oh, you can fly, can't you? Then I will throw you toward the nest so that you can fly back to the nest." She wrapped the little swallow in her hands, and threw him toward the nest, saying "One, two, three." The little swallow was thrown to where he could see the nest. He flapped his wings hard and grabbed its edge. The other little swallows got delighted and began to chirp. The flight attendant looked up at the nest, waved her hand and left for the airport building, saying "Be careful not to fall again."

The Adventure
of a Little Swallow

The calves think of the veterinarians as their fathers and the men and the women who clean their stable, brush and wash them as their mothers.

On the day when grown-up cattle or pigs are sent to their buyer, the veterinarians and the men and the women who have taken care of them see them off. Everybody wave their hands with tears in their eyes. The cattle and pigs make loud crying sounds, too. Some of the women start to sob. I felt tears running down my cheeks, too. My uncle put his hand on my head and said, " Good boy. You listen to your father and mother and study hard. Take good care of your parents." I made up my mind to do so, drying my tears.

When I got home, my mother was waiting for me. She had made ice cream for me. The moment I saw my mother, I couldn't help crying. So I went to the bathroom, wiped my tears away and washed my face. Then I ate the ice cream with my mother.

The End

shed. They put it into the soil as manure to produce better crops. Rice farmers bring straw to a stock farm after they harvest rice. The straw is mixed with dung so it will be used as manure. In this way, dairy farmers and rice farmers help each other by circulating dung and straw. This kind of farming is called recycling agriculture.

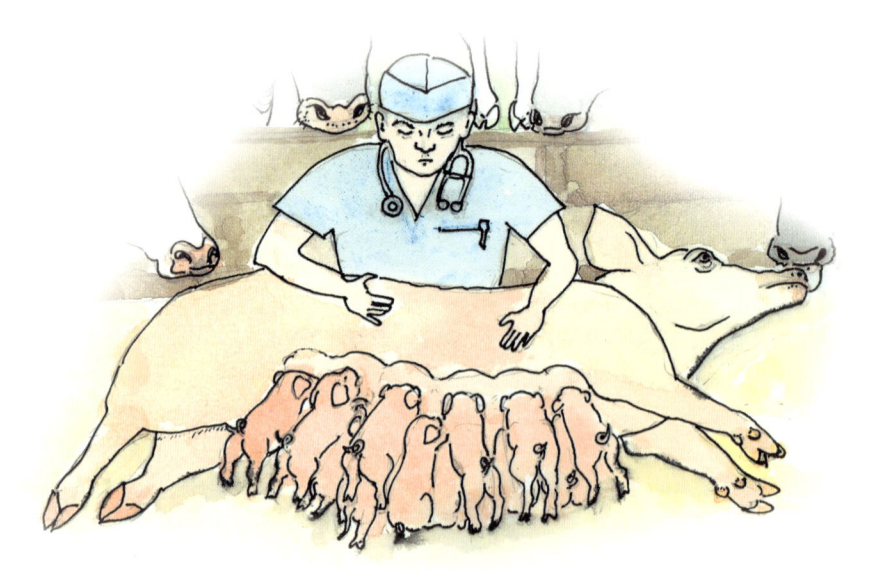

I think it's great that people who do different kind of jobs circulate unnecessary by-products between each other so that they can create useful things.

The calves in the stable wear a collar with a small computer on it. They suck at a huge nursing bottle placed in the stable. The bottle stops providing milk when they finish drinking just the suitable amount of milk for each of them so that they won't drink too much.

The veterinarians input information in computer programming to control the ingredients and the quantity of the milk that the calves drink. Each calf grows up by drinking the amount of milk controlled by the veterinarians.

My uncle, a Veterinarian

I'm in the sixth grade in elementary school. I went to the country to visit my uncle in the summer vacation.

My uncle is a veterinarian. He runs a stock farm with his friend who is also a veterinarian. They keep 3,000 head of cattle and 5,000 pigs.

My uncle has been fond of animals since he was a child. When he was in elementary school, he would often enjoy catching lizards and small snakes. He once told me how much he liked to see a snake straighten up when he put it on the ground and told it to straighten up, patting its back.

His mother would often be astonished by lizards or snakes that she found in the washing machine when she put his trousers in it. But she never blamed him for that.

She also liked animals, so a dog was kept at his house. The dog was more obedient to my uncle than to his mother who gave it food.

My uncle entered a college to become a veterinarian. As a student, he often had hard time taking care of horses and cattle. He was in trouble when huge and strong animals were disobedient or getting out of his control. He studied really hard, giving injections to cattle, horses, and pigs, having them take medicine, taking ray photographs of them, analyzing their urine, giving them a blood test, and studying in the library.

After passing the national examination for a veterinarian's license, My uncle had to decide what kind of job he was going to do. There are many kinds of jobs he could do as a veterinarian:taking care of sick or injured animals in a veterinary clinic in town or in a zoo, delivering babies of cows or pigs and milking cows on a farm, helping dogs stay in good condition while they receive training as a police dog or a guide dog, examining beef or pork at a health center, and so on.

After he got a veterinarian's license, My uncle worked in a veterinary clinic, and then asked a veterinarian at a zoo for advice, and finally made up his mind to work on a stock farm.

There are a lot of cattle and pigs on the farm. Whenever My uncle comes in the stable or the pig-cote, all the animals – both monstrous cattle or pigs and cute calves or young pigs – welcome him. They nod to him, make noises, or stick out their tongues. He strokes their heads or pats their necks, saying, "How are you?"

Since there are a lot of cattle on his farm, they produce a large amount of dung. The dung is collected by a bulldozer, mixed with straw, and is heaped in the

My uncle, a Veterinarian

The puppies kept growing bigger and bigger. Now they were about one meter withers height, nearly as big as their mother. They began to bark, "Guo". The cat also had learned to bark "Buo". The people at the hospital were amused to hear the cat barking. The nurses often said humorously, "The cat is going to bark."

The children in the pediatric ward enjoyed looking out the window at the barking cat in a tree. When they behaved badly, the nurses would often say, "The cat is going to bark at you." Then the children became obedient. Before long, the nurses began to say, "The cat is going to bark at you" to the grown-up patients as well as to the children.

"You have to try and eat more."

"But I don't have an appetite."

"The cat is going to bark at you."

"Then I'll have a little more."

People would often talk like this in the hospital.

"The cat is going to bark at you." These words made everybody happy and cheerful and surely helped the patients get better soon.

The End

kitten in there."

After the nurse left, Aki-chan went over to the window once again. The mother dog was nursing and licking the kitten as well as her own four pappies. Aki-chan was relieved to see that. But at the same time, he had some mysterious feelings.

Day by day, both the puppies and the kitten were growing and began to romp around happily together. The kitten was able to move much more quickly than the puppies. When one of the puppies tried to jump onto the kitten for fun, it ran away and climbed a tree. The puppies and the kitten began to bark, "Buo", by imitating their mother barking, "Guo".

As time went by, the puppies were getting bigger and bigger, while the kitten didn't grow very much. Whenever the guard took their mother for a walk, the puppies and the kitten came after her. The puppies tried to keep up with their mother, while the kitten jumped across the grass, climbed the tree, and barked on a tree. The guard was surprised to hear the cat barking.

The Cat is Going to Bark

There was once a Saint Bernard in a hospital on the outskirts of Osaka. The dog would follow the guard when he went around the hospital. Saint Bernards are dogs trained for rescuing mountain climbers in the Alps, Switzerland. They are very large, strong dogs, about one meter in withers height.

The dog was brought to the hospital from Switzerland for a Christmas present last year. That's why it was named Chris. However, the people at the hospital who cherished the dog — the nurses, the cooks and the janitors — preferred to call it "Ku-chan". The cage in the hospital yard was where the dog lived. The children who were in the pediatric ward were able to see the cage through the windows of their rooms. So they spent a lot of time watching the dog.

One day Ku-chan had four babies. The tiny cute puppies nestled against their mother's belly, searching for the breasts, sucking milk and sleeping peacefully. When their mother, Ku-chan licked them with her large tongue, they were rolling around and very excited.

Among the children in the pediatric ward was a ten-year-old boy, Aki-chan, who was bright and very fond of animals. One day while looking out the window at the cage, Aki-chan noticed something unusual about the dogs. There seemed to be another white puppy that he had never seen. As the other four puppies were covered with brown spots like their mother, it was easy to tell the difference. Aki-chan told one of the nurses about it. Looking out the window, she said, "That's kind of strange. I'll ask the janitor to go and see what is going on with the dogs. So, you stay in bed, will you?" She patted him on the head gently, put him to bed, and left the room.

Lying in bed, Aki-chan was wondering about the dogs for a while. Then he went over to the window to see what was happening down there. The janitor was standing outside the cage watching the dogs. Aki-chan was glad to know that the nurse had kept her word, so he kept watching even more closely. Though the janitor tried to get into the cage, Ku-chan scared him away by barking fiercely. He couldn't possibly enter the cage. Aki-chan was watching them anxiously.

Before long, the nurse came back and said, "Go back to bed now, and I'll tell you what I've found out." Putting him to bed, she said, "You see, there seemed to be four puppies and a white kitten there." Aki-chan was surprised to hear that and said, "Did the dog give birth to the kitten?" The nurse said laughing, "That's impossible. Dogs give birth to only dogs. Someone must have brought and left the

The Cat is Going to Bark

CONTENTS

The Cat is Going to Bark · · · · · · · · · · · · · i

My uncle, a Veterinarian · · · · · · · · · · · · · v

The Adventure of a Little Swallow · · · · · · ix

Yuko-chan and Jogging · · · · · · · · · · · · · xiii

あとがき

最近は従来の常識では考えられない事件が多くなりました。皆が忙しくて、祖父母、両親、兄弟姉妹などが仲良く、和やかに、話をする機会が少なくなったためかと思います。

技術革新、コンピューター時代の影響など原因を議論するよりも、皆で和やかに話をする機会を作る方法の一つとしてこの本を作ってみました。

御両親や兄弟姉妹、皆で読んで、幼い子供達も一緒に微笑みながらお話をされる機会が出来ればと願っております。

日英両文に致しました。海外へのホームステイや留学などに行く人達、外国から日本に来られる人も多く、小学校で英語の授業が始まり、看護師さんや介護士さんなど海外からの受け入れが始まる時代、色々の場でお役に立つことを期待しております。

平成二十年八月　執筆者一同

作者プロフィール

赤松 清：元旭化成㈱研究所
　　　　　元㈶生産開発科学研究所 評議員
　　　　　おもな著書、『光成形シートの製造と応用』『新しい時代の感光性樹脂』『帯電防止材料の最新技術と応用展開』他多数
　　他：ご家族、ご友人一同

この童話は、長年、感光性樹脂をはじめとした高分子科学の研究に携わり、また人間の豊かな暮らしを目指し技術の発展に貢献してきた研究者が、「もの（技術）」から「心（文章）」へと表現の形を変えた作品です。

ニャンニャンがほえるぞ
―The Cat is Going to Bark―

2008年9月30日　第1刷発行　　　　　　　　　　（B0867）

著　者　（文）赤松　清・幸子　（英訳）つじ　もとこ
　　　　（絵）赤松　茂・赤松　学
発行者　辻　賢司
発行所　株式会社シーエムシー出版
　　　　東京都千代田区内神田1-13-1（豊島屋ビル）
　　　　電話 03 (3293) 2061
　　　　大阪市中央区南新町1-2-4（椿本ビル）
　　　　電話 06 (4794) 8234
　　　　http://www.cmcbooks.co.jp/

〔印刷　株式会社遊文舎〕　　　　　　　　　　Ⓒ K. Akamatsu, 2008

定価はカバーに表示してあります。
落丁・乱丁本はお取替えいたします。

本書の内容の一部あるいは全部を無断で複写（コピー）することは、法律で認められた場合を除き、著作者および出版社の権利の侵害になります。

ISBN978-4-7813-0050-4　C8093　¥1200E